# THE JUNGLE BOOK

W9-AHA-407

## by RUDYARD KIPLING

# #4 Mowgli
# Knows Best

Adapted by Diane Namm

Illustrated by Nathan Hale

**Sterling Publishing Co., Inc.**
New York

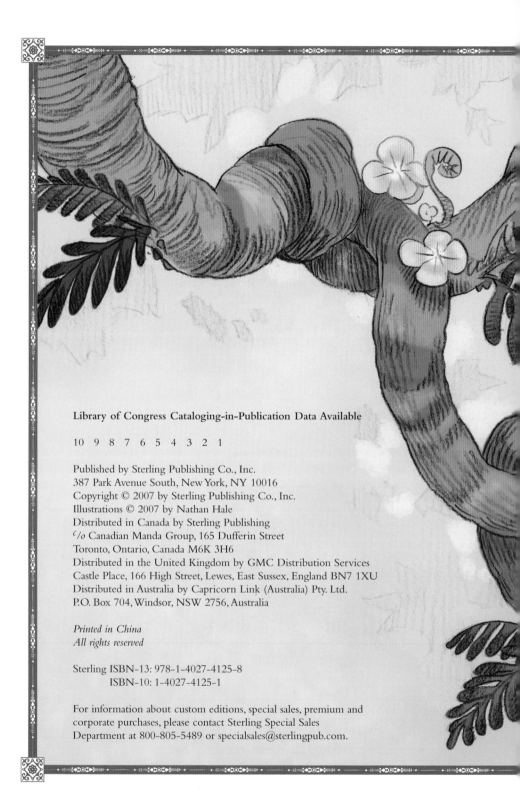

Library of Congress Cataloging-in-Publication Data Available

10  9  8  7  6  5  4  3  2  1

Published by Sterling Publishing Co., Inc.
387 Park Avenue South, New York, NY 10016
Copyright © 2007 by Sterling Publishing Co., Inc.
Illustrations © 2007 by Nathan Hale
Distributed in Canada by Sterling Publishing
c/o Canadian Manda Group, 165 Dufferin Street
Toronto, Ontario, Canada M6K 3H6
Distributed in the United Kingdom by GMC Distribution Services
Castle Place, 166 High Street, Lewes, East Sussex, England BN7 1XU
Distributed in Australia by Capricorn Link (Australia) Pty. Ltd.
P.O. Box 704, Windsor, NSW 2756, Australia

*Printed in China*
*All rights reserved*

Sterling ISBN-13: 978-1-4027-4125-8
        ISBN-10: 1-4027-4125-1

For information about custom editions, special sales, premium and
corporate purchases, please contact Sterling Special Sales
Department at 800-805-5489 or specialsales@sterlingpub.com.

# Contents

## Mowgli Disappears

Mowgli and his friends
Bagheera, the panther, and
Baloo, the bear, had traveled
through the jungle for many weeks.
Bagheera and Baloo
showed Mowgli how to
live safely in the jungle.
But Mowgli did not listen.

"If you see the tiger Shere Khan, climb a tree!" said Baloo.

"Why should I?" asked Mowgli.

"I would rather stay and fight!"

"If you see Kaa, the rock snake,"
said Bagheera, "run away
as fast as you can!"
"You look funny!" Mowgli laughed.

"Mowgli, stop!" Bagheera said.

"I want to play," said Mowgli.

Baloo and Bagheera

just shook their heads.

"This is your fault," said Baloo.

"You spoil him," growled Bagheera.

"You never let him play!" said Baloo.

"The jungle is not a playground!" Bagheera roared.

Baloo and Bagheera were
so busy shouting, they did
not see Mowgli creep away.

"Where is Mowgli?" asked Baloo.

"He was right here," Bagheera said.

They did not see Mowgli anywhere.

"We must find him," said Baloo.

"Mowgli! Where are you?" they called.

Mowgli didn't hear them, but

Shere Khan, the tiger, and

Kaa, the rock snake, heard them well.

## Bad Company

Baloo and Bagheera
crashed through the jungle.
Baloo stopped, "Listen!" he said.
Then Bagheera heard it, too.
"It is the giggle sound that
only Mowgli makes," said Baloo.
"If we can hear it, so can
Shere Khan," worried Bagheera.

Mowgli was with the monkeys,
who laughed and played all day.
He liked them very much.
They liked Mowgli, too.

"There he is!" cried Bagheera.

"Quick, save him!" said Baloo.

"Hold on, Mowgli," they shouted,

"We're coming to rescue you!"

"I don't want to leave!"
Mowgli shook his head.
"I want to stay here and
have fun," he said.

"The monkeys will play
tricks on you," growled Bagheera.
"That's not true!" Mowgli said.
"Stop this, Mowgli!" said Baloo.

Before Baloo and Bagheera
could take Mowgli away,
the monkeys scooped him
up and carried him off.

## Big Trouble!

Mowgli showed off for the
monkeys all day long.
He did somersaults and cartwheels
while they clapped and laughed.
They never said, "Mowgli, stop!"
When Mowgli was done,
the monkeys were bored.
They looked for something else to do.

The monkeys spotted
Kaa, the rock snake, sleeping
on a rock in the sun.
"Let's play a trick," they said.

While Kaa was fast asleep,
the monkeys laughed
as they tied him into tight knots
and hung him over a tree limb.

"You'll hurt him!" Mowgli told them.

The monkeys just ignored him.

"That's not funny," Mowgli said.

"Yes it is!" they laughed.

Mowgli waited for the monkeys
to go somewhere else to play.
Slowly, gently, he untied the knots,
just as Kaa began to wake.

"What are you doing, man-cub?"
Kaa asked Mowgli with a hiss.

"Untying you," Mowgli said.

"Aren't you afraid?" asked Kaa.

"Nothing scares me," said Mowgli.

"Is that so?" Kaa hissed.

"Run, Mowgli, run!" Baloo cried.

"Let the man-cub go, Kaa,"
Bagheera snarled angrily.

"Wait!" shouted Mowgli,
"He is my friend!"
"What?" asked Bagheera.
"Who?" asked Baloo.
"Me!" hissed Kaa with an evil smile.

# Friends and Enemies

Baloo and Bagheera could
not believe their ears.

"Kaa is no one's friend," Baloo said.

"He is, too!" Mowgli said.

"He is not!" Bagheera growled.

While they argued, Kaa tightened
his coils around Mowgli and smiled.

"At last! The man-cub is mine!"
Shere Khan the tiger roared.
He leaped from the bushes,
heading straight for the boy.

"Give me the man-cub, Kaa!"
Shere Khan roared.

"Never!" hissed Kaa, "He's mine!"

"Leave us!" growled Baloo.

"Now!" Bagheera roared.

"Let me fight, too!" cried Mowgli,
"You see? You are outnumbered.
"Four of us against you!" hissed Kaa.

Shere Khan looked from one
enemy to the other.
"I'll be back," he growled, and
slouched off into the jungle.

"Let the man-cub go," growled Baloo.

"Why should I?" Kaa hissed back.

"We say so," roared Bagheera.

Slowly Kaa unwound his coils.

"I hope you learned your lesson
this time," Baloo began to say.
"Where is he?" asked Bagheera.
Then they heard the sound
that only Mowgli makes.
They looked at each other.
They started to run.
"Here we go again!"